OTHER YEARLING BOOKS YOU WILL ENJOY:

CLUES IN THE WOODS, *Peggy Parish*
HAUNTED HOUSE, *Peggy Parish*
HAVE YOU SEEN HYACINTH MACAW?, *Patricia Reilly Giff*
THE EGYPT GAME, *Zilpha Keatley Snyder*
THE DIAMOND WAR, *Zilpha Keatley Snyder*
THE GYPSY GAME, *Zilpha Keatley Snyder*
THE HEADLESS CUPID, *Zilpha Keatley Snyder*
LIBBY ON WEDNESDAY, *Zilpha Keatley Snyder*
BOX TOP DREAMS, *Miriam Glassman*
GHOST OF A CHANCE, *Laura Peyton Roberts*

YEARLING BOOKS are designed especially to entertain and enlighten young people. Patricia Reilly Giff, consultant to this series, received her bachelor's degree from Marymount College and a master's degree in history from St. John's University. She holds a Professional Diploma in Reading and a Doctorate of Humane Letters from Hofstra University. She was a teacher and reading consultant for many years, and is the author of numerous books for young readers.

Key to the Treasure

by
Peggy Parish
illustrated by
Paul Frame

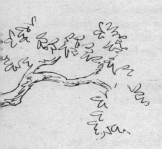

A YEARLING BOOK

For Kathleen Daly

Published by
Bantam Doubleday Dell Books for Young Readers
a division of
Bantam Doubleday Dell Publishing Group, Inc.
1540 Broadway
New York, New York 10036

ISBN: 0-440-44438-1

Reprinted by arrangement with Macmillan Publishing Co., Inc.

Printed in the United States of America

April 1980

OPM 42 41 40 39 38 37 36 35

Contents

Summer Plans

"Hey, there's Grandpa now," said Jed. "Let's go ask him."

Jed, Bill, and Liza Roberts ran toward the porch where their grandfather was standing.

"Oh, there you are," said Grandpa. "I was just about to call you. Gran wants you to wash up for supper."

"Supper! Oh boy," said Bill.

"Grandpa," said Liza, "we need to talk to you."

"All right," said Grandpa, "but how about getting ready for supper first. Can't keep Gran waiting, you know."

The children quickly washed their hands and sat down at the table.

"Now, what was it you wanted to talk to me about?" asked Grandpa.

"A tree house," said Jed. "We found the most terrific place in the old oak for a tree house. Is it all right if we build one?"

"Certainly," said Grandpa. "That old tree hasn't held a tree house since your father was a boy. I expect it would be mighty pleased to hold another one."

"And Grandpa," said Liza, "do you think we could put up a rope? Then we could use it to swing from the house to the ground."

Grandpa chuckled. "You sound just like your father. Yes, you may have a rope. But I'll get Mr. Sanders to come over and put it up properly. I don't want any of you getting hurt."

"Gee, thanks, Grandpa," said Jed.

"Isn't anybody interested in eating?" asked Gran.

"I sure am!" said Bill.

"So am I," said Liza.

Everybody settled down to enjoy Gran's good supper.

Finally Bill pushed back his chair and said, "I'm stuffed. What do you say we start on the tree house now?"

"Now!" said everybody.

"Sure, why not?" asked Bill.

"Take a look out of the window," said Jed.

"Gee," said Bill, "didn't it get dark awfully early?"

"There's a cloud coming up," said Grandpa. "I think we'll get some rain before too long."

Gran began to clear away the dishes.

"Don't worry about the dishes," said Liza. "We'll do them."

3

"Oh, let's do them together," said Gran. "After all, this is your first night here."

Liza threw her arms around Gran and said, "It's so good to be here again. I thought summer vacation would never come."

"If you think you had a hard time waiting," said Grandpa, "you should have seen Gran. She started getting your rooms ready two weeks ago."

"I wish you lived right next door," said Bill. "It's such a long time from one summer to the next."

"That it is," said Gran, "but your Grandpa and I feel we're very lucky. Not all grandparents get to have their grandchildren with them three months every year."

Gran smiled at her "almost triplets" grandchildren. She called them that because they were so close in age. Jed was not

4

BILL

LIZA

JED

quite a year old when the twins, Liza and
Bill, were born.

"I just wish Mom and Dad could have
the whole summer too," said Liza.

"Yes," said Grandpa, "that would be
nice. But folks do have to work. Anyway,
they have an extra week this summer, so

they'll have a nice long visit with us."

With Gran's help, the dishes were done quickly and the kitchen was tidied up. Gran, Grandpa, and the three children went into the living room.

"My, it's getting chilly," said Gran. "I do believe a little fire would feel good."

"How about you boys bringing in some wood," said Grandpa. "The way that thunder is rumbling, I think we may have a bit of a storm. It might get really cool before this evening is over."

Bill and Jed hurried to the woodshed. They loaded up with wood and hurried back. The sound of the thunder was getting closer and closer.

Grandpa laid the wood and lit the fire. Liza watched the little blue flames lick the dry wood and grow into bigger flames.

Suddenly there came a sharp flash of lightning. It was followed by a loud clap of

thunder. The lights flickered. They flickered several times. Then they went out
altogether.

"A line must be down somewhere," said
Grandpa. "Are the lamps filled with oil?"

"Yes," said Gran, "I always keep them
ready in the cupboard. I can get them."

Gran could see well enough by the fire-

7

light to get to the cupboard. She took down two old-fashioned oil lamps and lit them. Their soft light filled the room.

There was another sharp flash of lightning. A heavy crash joined the boom of thunder that followed.

Liza ran to Gran.

"Too big to sit on your Gran's lap?" asked Gran.

"No!" said Liza. She slipped onto Gran's lap and put her head on Gran's shoulder.

"That lightning hit something—and very close by," said Grandpa.

"It came from toward the front," said Gran.

"Well, it couldn't have been the barn," said Grandpa, "but I should go check on the animals anyway."

"No," said Gran, "wait until this passes over."

Grandpa looked out of the window. The

8

rain was coming down in torrents. He decided Gran was right.

Jed lay on his back, looking at the picture above the mantel. It wasn't a real picture. It was just four pen-and-ink sketches. The first sketch was of a feathered Indian bonnet. The next was a small clay pot with a lid on it. The third sketch was a key. It was a strange-looking key that had a hook at the end. And last of all was a large question mark. The picture had hung in the same place for many and many a year.

"Grandpa," said Jed, "tell us the story of the picture."

"The story of the picture!" said Grandpa. "You children must know that by heart. I've told it to you so many times."

"But you haven't told it this summer," said Liza. "And besides that, you always remember something new that you haven't told us about."

Old Jane

Grandpa chuckled. "All right, you win. But this time I think I'll tell you two stories."

"Two stories!" said Liza.

"Well," said Grandpa, "it's really only one story. But I've never told you the first part."

"What do you mean?" asked Bill.

"You'll see," said Grandpa. And while the thunder rumbled and the lightning flashed outside, Grandpa began the story.

"A very long time ago, when my grand-father was just a small boy, an old Indian woman lived on their place. Nobody knew much about her. She had lived there as long as anyone could remember. She had worked hard all her life. When she began to grow old, my grandfather's family made sure she had everything she needed.

"My grandfather loved to go to her cabin. It was filled with Indian things, and Old Jane—that's what they called her—never seemed to tire of answering my grandfather's questions. Old Jane was always sewing. She tanned deer skins into the softest leather and made shirts for my grandfather and his father. While she sewed, she told my grandfather stories about her people.

"There was a feathered bonnet hanging on one wall of Old Jane's cabin. Grandfather begged and begged to try it on. But Old Jane never would let him. She told him that the time had not come for him to wear that. But she promised that someday he could put it on. And she always said that when she died he was to have all of the things of her people.

"My grandfather never missed a day going to see Old Jane. One day when he was about twelve years old he went to the cabin as usual. There was Old Jane sitting in her chair. Her hands were folded in her lap. My grandfather ran to her. He had never seen her when she wasn't busy. But Old Jane smiled at him when he came near. She told him to fetch the feathered bonnet. He brought it to her. Old Jane took it and told him to kneel down. Then, without a word, Old Jane placed the feathered bonnet on his head. She kissed both of his cheeks and motioned for him to go.

"That was the last time Grandfather saw Old Jane alive."

All three children were silent. Finally Liza said, "Oh, Grandpa, I'm glad you didn't send the feathered bonnet to the museum with the other Indian things."

"As a matter of fact, we almost did," said Grandpa. "When we decided to let the museum borrow the collection, Gran and I packed the feathered bonnet, too. But then, at the last minute, we just couldn't let it go. The men were here and beginning to take the boxes out. Gran ran and stopped them. We both rushed to the box that held the feathered bonnet and took it out. We put it back in the case in the hall. It had always been there, and there it's stayed ever since."

"I do see what you mean about that story," said Bill. "It had to happen before the story of the picture could happen."

14

The Story of the Picture

"That story," said Grandpa, "begins many years later. My grandfather had built this house. He had a wife and three children of his own.

"My grandfather was a fun-loving man and was always making up new games for his children to enjoy. Of course, they knew the story of Old Jane and the Indian collection. One of their favorite games was choosing the things from the collection they would most like to have for their own. Grandfather told them that when they were old enough to really take care of them, they could have the things they wanted. My fa-

15

ther had his eye on a leather war shield that had a picture of an Indian battle painted on it. Then there was a doll made from deerskin that Aunt Mary had her heart set on. The doll had real hair and a deerskin dress, and wore little beaded moccasins. Aunt Mary told me about that doll and how much she wanted it many a time. In the collection there was also a ferocious-looking mask that was used to scare away evil spirits. Aunt Mary used to shudder when she told me about that. But that was the thing Uncle Frank most wanted."

"Yes," said Bill, "that's for me."

Bill got up and began dancing around making weird noises.

"You don't need a mask to scare things," said Liza. She covered her ears.

"Oh sit down," said Jed. "Let Grandpa tell the story."

"Of course, there were other things the

children wanted, but those were their extra-special choices. They all wanted the fea-thered bonnet, but Grandfather said that that was his special choice.

"The Civil War was going on, and Grand-father knew he would soon have to join the fighting. His children were very unhappy about this. They didn't want their father to go away. Grandfather couldn't stand seeing his children unhappy. He decided to leave them something to keep them busy and amused while he was away. He left them a puzzle to solve.

"Early on the morning he was to go, he called his family together. He told the children he was going to see how clever they were. He had hidden clues for them to fol-low that would lead them to a treasure. Grandfather held up a small envelope. He said that the whereabouts of the first clue was inside. He started to give the envelope

18

to the children. But Grandmother stopped him. She said that if he gave it to the children then they wouldn't do their chores and she needed their help with him going away. Grandfather and the children knew better than to argue with Grandmother. She was a real stickler for work. And no matter what the situation was, work must come before play. Nothing could change Grandmother's mind about that! So Grandfather handed Grandmother the envelope. She dropped it into her apron pocket.

"Grandfather winked at the children and told them they would just have to do their chores extra fast. The children were terribly excited. They asked if the treasure was hidden in the house. Grandfather told them it was hidden in a part of the house. They asked if they could look for the treasure without the clues. He told them yes, but he didn't think they could find it. And he was

sure they wouldn't find the first clue without the envelope.

"But the children still weren't satisfied.
They begged him to give them just a hint.
He laughed and said that he didn't think
their mother would object to just a hint. It
might make them work faster. He left the
room, and when he came back he had a flat
package under his arm. He told the children that they could open it as soon as he

had ridden as far as the bend in the road. What was in the package would give them their hint.

"Then they went out on the porch and Grandfather kissed each of them good-bye. He got on his horse and rode away.

"But before Grandfather had rounded the bend, a man came riding in from the other direction. The man told Grandmother that her sister was ill and wanted her please to come. This upset everybody. While the man hitched up the horse to the buggy, Grandmother packed a few clothes. Then she bundled the children into the buggy and off they went.

"Grandmother's sister didn't live too many miles away, but it was a long trip in those days. There were no paved roads, and the horse couldn't go very fast pulling a buggy.

"It was more than a week before Grandmother's sister was well enough for Grandmother to bring the children back home. It was night when they got back, and the children were tired out. Grandmother put them right to bed.

"Early the next morning the children got up. Their first thought was the treasure. Quickly they opened the package their father had left. They saw the four sketches he

had made. When they recognized the sketch of the feathered bonnet, they ran to the case where the bonnet was kept. They looked it over carefully, but it looked the same as it always had. The children were puzzled. Then Aunt Mary recognized the little pot as being one from the Indian collection. They rushed back to the collection. And they found that the little pot was gone. Not only was the pot gone, but so were all of their special choices. The children were so excited they couldn't stand it another minute. They decided to try to get their mother to give them the envelope right away.

"The children ran to the kitchen and began clamoring for the envelope. Grandmother had been so upset about everything that she had thought no more about the envelope. When she heard the children, she threw up her hands and ran out the back door. The children could not imagine what was wrong. Never had they seen their mother act that way. They ran after her. Then they knew. Grandmother was doing the laundry. There was a big tub of clothes boiling. And in that tub was the apron with the envelope. Grandmother took a stick and fished the apron out of the tub. But it was too late. The note was nothing but a pulpy mess. Of course, there was nothing that could be done about it.

"The children began looking for their father to come home. Some of the other men had already returned. But Grandfather never came back. He was killed in some last-minute fighting.

"The children had looked everywhere they could think of. They studied the picture over and over again. Since the first sketch was of a feathered bonnet, they thought maybe the clue was there. They took the bonnet down again and again, but they couldn't find a sign of a clue. They practically took the house apart looking for the treasure. But it was no use. The things were never found."

A Late Good-night

"Gee," said Liza, "it makes me feel all sad to think about those children looking so hard for the treasure and never finding it."

"I know," said Grandpa. "When I was a little boy and my father would tell me that story, I would feel the same way. More than anything in the world, I wanted to find that treasure and surprise him."

Suddenly Jed smiled. He looked at Liza and Bill. Then all three children started to laugh.

Grandpa looked puzzled. He said, "And what's wrong with wanting to surprise your father?"

"Nothing, Grandpa," said Jed. "But that's exactly what Dad said. More than anything in the world, when he was a little boy, he wanted to find that treasure and surprise you!"

"Oh, he did, did he! I never knew that," said Grandpa. He chuckled. "That's a good one on me."

"Your Grandpa and I thought for sure it would turn up when we put in electricity and water," said Gran. "We followed the workmen every step. But we didn't find a thing."

"Gee, Grandpa," said Jed, "do you think the things would be any good now if they were found?"

"That depends on where my grandfather hid them. If they are in a dry place, they'll be all right. Just recently I read about them finding a little horse made of twigs that was three thousand years old."

"I wish we could find the treasure. How I would love to have that doll," said Liza. "Oh, if we just had one little clue."

Grandpa chuckled and pointed to the picture. He said, "There's your clue. All you have to do is figure out what it means."

Just then the lights came back on.

"That's a surprise," said Grandpa. "I didn't think we would have lights again tonight."

"I'm glad they're on," said Gran. "We

can have some hot chocolate. Everybody will sleep better."

"I'm for your hot chocolate anytime," said Bill.

"You're for food anytime," said Jed.

Grandpa put on his raincoat and got a flashlight.

"While you fix it, I'll just check on the animals," he said.

By the time the hot chocolate was ready, Grandpa was back.

"Everything's fine out back," he said.

"Could you see what the lightning hit?" asked Bill.

"No," said Grandpa. "It is raining too hard to scout around. That will have to wait until morning."

After the hot chocolate everybody said their good-nights and went to bed. It was way past bedtime. The children fell asleep almost as soon as they lay down.

Spoiled Plans

When Liza woke up the next morning it was gray and overcast.

"Oh, no," she said. "It looks as if it might rain any minute."

She quickly dressed and ran downstairs. Jed and Bill were already eating breakfast.

"Hi, Lazybones," said Bill.

"Hi. Where's Grandpa?" asked Liza.

"He had his breakfast earlier," said Gran. "He went out to take a look around."

"Hurry up, Liza," said Jed, "we want to get started on the tree house."

"I think it's going to rain," said Liza.

"But we can work until it does," said Bill.

"Why don't we go ahead and find the board and tools," said Jed.

Just as he said that, Grandpa came in.

"I'm afraid you children will have to wait a day or so to start your tree house," he said.

"Why?" they all asked.

"Lightning," said Grandpa. "It hit one of the big limbs in the top of the old oak. The limb is wedged up in the tree."

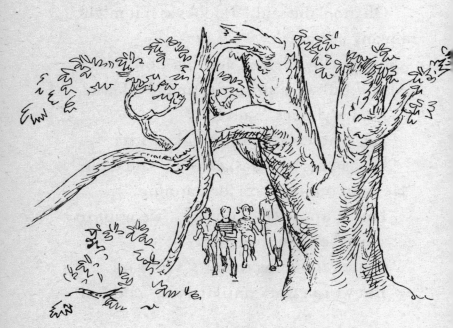

The children did not wait to hear more. They left the table and raced out of the house. Gran and Grandpa followed them.

"Oh, I hope it's not one of our limbs," said Liza.

"But it looks as if it is," said Bill.

Jed went closer.

He called, "Nope, we're okay. That limb is just hanging down over ours."

Liza and Bill went closer too.

"Thank goodness," said Liza. "All three of the limbs we wanted are still there."

"Grandpa, can't we just break off the lower part of it and go on with our tree house?" asked Bill.

"Indeed not!" said Grandpa. "That's a big limb. Any movement might bring it down on you. I'll not have you take that kind of a chance."

"How long do you think we'll have to wait?" asked Jed.

"I'll call Mr. Sanders today," said Grandpa. "He has the proper equipment to do things like that. It will depend on when he has the time to do it. I'll get him to put up your rope swing at the same time."

"Well, there go our plans for today," said Liza.

"But we can still look for the boards and things we need, can't we, Grandpa?" asked Bill.

"Sure," said Grandpa. "I don't think you would get much more than that done today anyway. That rain is coming soon."

The children went out back where Grandpa kept scrap lumber. They began plundering in the pile, pulling out boards they thought they could use.

Liza picked up a piece and some black bugs ran out.

"Ugh, bugs!" she said.

32

"Sure, there're always bugs around old wood," said Bill. He picked one up.

"Here, get acquainted with it," he said and put the bug on Liza's arm.

"You stop that, Bill!" screamed Liza. "You're just being mean."

Then the rain started. The children ran

to the house. But they were damp by the time they got there anyway.

"Rain caught up with you, I see," said Grandpa.

"Run on up and change," said Grandma. "It's too chilly to stay in wet clothes today."

The children went up to their rooms and changed into dry clothes.

The Lucky Fight

The rain settled down to slow mist. It wasn't really raining, but it was too unpleasant to be out. Grandpa had business in town, so he was gone. The children helped Gran shell beans. Then they played games. But they were too restless and disappointed at not being able to be outdoors to stick with anything for very long.

Late that afternoon Bill remembered the feathered bonnet.

"Let's try on the Indian bonnet. We haven't done that this summer," he said.

"Better ask Gran first," said Jed.

"I'll ask her," said Liza. She went into the kitchen.

"Gran, is it all right if we try on the Indian bonnet?" asked Liza.

"Yes," said Gran. "But do be careful with it. Remember, it is very old."

"Don't worry," said Liza, "we'll be very careful."

The children took the bonnet from the glass case where it hung.

"Let's take it upstairs," said Jed. "There's more room to play there."

Bill put the bonnet on, and they followed him to the boys' room.

"Say, I make a pretty good Indian," said Bill. He began to dance around in front of the mirror.

"It's my turn now," said Liza. "You've had it long enough."

Bill paid no attention to her. He went right on dancing around and making all sorts of weird sounds.

"That's no fair, Bill," said Liza. "Stop it right now."

"Watch out," said Bill, "I'll scalp you."

Bill ran around the bed. Liza was angry. She ran after Bill, and he jumped across the

bed. Liza reached out to grab him. But instead she caught the end of the bonnet. Bill went right on. When Liza looked down, she was horrified. There in her hand was the big black feather that should have been on the end of the bonnet.

"Look what you made me do!" screamed Liza. "And I promised Gran we would be careful."

"I didn't make you do that," said Bill. "You grabbed the bonnet."

"Well, it wouldn't have happened if you had played fair," said Liza.

"It's no use fighting about it now," said Jed. "We better find a way to fix it. Do you think we can paste the feather back in?"

Liza looked at the feather in her hand.

"We can try," she said. "I have some paste."

Liza went to her room and got the paste. When she got back, Jed was studying the bonnet.

"This will be easy to fix," he said. "See, each feather fits into its own pocket. Those people sure did a lot of work to make these bonnets."

Liza looked for the pocket in which the

38

black feather belonged. She saw something sticking a tiny bit out of it.

"That looks like a piece of paper," she said. "Did the Indians use paper to make their bonnets?"

"Never heard of them doing that," said Bill. "Take it out."

Liza pulled, and a folded piece of paper came out of the pocket.

"It sure is paper," said Jed. "See if it has anything written on it."

Liza tried to unfold the paper. A corner tore off.

"Gee, this must be old," she said. "Look how brittle it is."

She tried again to unfold it. But everytime she touched the paper, a piece broke off.

"Maybe we better paste the pieces onto another piece of paper," said Jed. "We'll never find out anything this way."

Bill took the paste.

"Are you going to do the pasting?" asked Liza.

"Yes," said Bill. "I'm pretty good at this kind of thing."

"It does have something written on it!" said Liza. "I can see some letters."

"I hope it's not written in Indian," said Bill.

The children were so excited they could hardly sit still. But they worked carefully until the last piece of paper was pasted into place.

"What does it say?" asked Liza. "Oh, do hurry!"

Bill read, " 'All twenty-six. This is your first clue.' "

"Grandpa's grandfather!" shouted Liza. "We've found it! We've found it!"

"Shh," said Jed.

"Why are you shushing me?" asked Liza.

"Let's keep it a secret until we find out what it is," said Jed.

"Yes, let's do!" said Bill. "Maybe we can surprise Grandpa by finding the treasure ourselves."

"Well, we've got the first clue," said Liza, "but what on earth does it mean?"

"That's what we have to find out," said Jed.

The children looked at the paper. They were puzzled. Below the words was a whole list of numbers.

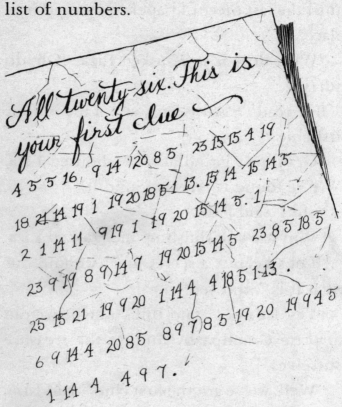

All twenty-six. This is your first clue

4 5 5 16   9 14 20 8 5   23 15 15 4 19

18 21 14 19 1 19 20 18 5 1 13. 15 14   5 14 3

2 1 14 11   9 19 1   19 20 15 14 5.   1

23 9 19 8 9 14 7   19 20 15 14 5   23 8 5 18 5

25 15 21   19 9 20   1 14 4   4 18 5 1 13 .

6 9 14 4   20 8 5   8 9 7 8 5 19 20   19 4 4 5

1 14 4   4 9 7 .

"Liza, Jed, Bill," called Gran, "come on down to supper."

"Coming, Gran," called Bill. Nobody ever had to call him to eat twice, no matter what the situation was.

"Now remember," said Jed, "secret's the word." He put the piece of paper in the desk drawer.

"Oh, the bonnet," said Liza. "We forgot about the bonnet."

"I'll fix that right quick," said Bill. He put some paste on the end of the black feather and stuck the feather into the empty pocket.

"I hope it stays," said Jed.

"It will," said Bill. He picked up the bonnet and took it downstairs. Liza helped him put it back in the case.

Bill grinned at Liza. He said, "Well, twin sister, that fight sure turned out to be worth having."

Liza stuck out her tongue at Bill. Then they both giggled and went in to supper.

An Idea in the Night

Supper seemed to last forever. Then there were the dishes to do.

"I wish Gran would get a dishwasher," said Bill. "How does she ever manage to use so many things for one little meal?"

"You'd be the first to complain if she didn't fix a lot of food," said Jed. "Anyway, we're about through."

Liza washed out the sink while the boys put the dishes away. They had just finished when Gran called.

"The Reverend and Mrs. Jenks are here," said Gran. "They very much want to see you."

44

"Wouldn't you know it?" said Bill. "To-night of all nights."

"Maybe they won't stay very long," said Liza.

"Well, let's go and get it over with," said Jed.

The children went out on the porch.

"There you are," said Reverend Jenks. "It is nice to have you back again."

The children shook hands with the Reverend and his wife. Then they sat in the swing.

"We have all sorts of plans for the summer," said Reverend Jenks. "We hope to start a softball team. Jed, do you and Bill play?"

"Yes, sir," said Jed.

"Good, we'll need you. Then there's the Sunday-school picnic," the Reverend went on.

At any other time the children would

have been excited about all of this. They liked the Reverend and Mrs. Jenks, and they enjoyed Sunday school. But tonight they had other things to think about. "All twenty-six" kept going around in their minds. They were very quiet.

Finally Gran said, "Come Liza, help me fix some lemonade."

Liza went into the kitchen with Gran.

"What is the matter with you three tonight? You've hardly said a word," said Gran.

"I guess we're just tired," said Liza. "And with the rain and not being able to work on the tree house—it's been such a long day."

"Yes, it has been quite a day," said Gran. "I'm tired myself."

Gran carried the pitcher of lemonade and some glasses out to the porch. Liza followed with a tray of cookies.

After she served the lemonade, Gran told the Reverend and Mrs. Jenks about the bro-

ken limb on the old oak and the spoiled
plans for making a tree house.

"That old oak is a fine place for a tree
house," said Reverend Jenks. "I remember
one your father and I made when we were
boys. We had your grandfather help us put
up a long pipe. We slid down the pipe from
the tree house to the ground. Do you remember that, Mr. Roberts?"

"Indeed I do," said Grandpa. He chuckled and said, "If I remember correctly, you boys let me have the first turn sliding down as payment for helping you."

Everybody laughed at that.

"And," added Grandpa, "you boys were pretty good at shinnying up the pipe, too."

"Gee," said Jed, "that sounds like fun."

"Say, Grandpa," said Bill, "do you think you could help us put up a pipe?"

"I expect I could still manage that kind of thing," said Grandpa.

"We promise you can have the first turn," said Liza.

"Then I know I can do it," said Grandpa.

Liza ran to Grandpa and hugged him.

Soon after that, the Reverend and Mrs. Jenks said their good-nights and left.

"All right," said Gran, "off to bed with you three."

"Bed!" said Bill. "This early!"

"You were up very late last night," said Gran. "Liza was just saying how tired you all are."

The children started upstairs.

"You sure fixed that up," said Bill.

"What else could I say?" asked Liza. "Gran wanted to know what was wrong with us. I really think we should tell them."

"No," said Jed. "This will be a lot more exciting if we can do it by ourselves. Matter of fact, I am tired."

He pulled Liza's hair as he went by and said, "Dream about the puzzle. We couldn't do anything tonight anyway."

Liza found to her surprise that she was yawning. She, too, was ready for bed.

All of the children went to sleep quickly.

Later in the night, Liza woke up. She sat up in bed.

" 'All twenty-six'—the alphabet! That's it!" she said.

She turned on her lamp and slipped out of bed. Liza went into the hall. Slowly she made her way to the boys' room.

"Jed, Bill," she whispered, "wake up, I know the answer."

Neither boy moved. Jed was closer. Liza shook him. He turned over.

"Jed, it's the alphabet. 'All twenty-six' means the alphabet," said Liza.

"Alphabet, phooey," mumbled Jed. "Go away."

"Huh," said Bill, and he made some queer sounds.

Liza sighed. It was just no use. When her brothers slept, nothing could get them up. She went back to her room.

Liza softly closed her door so that her light wouldn't awaken Gran or Grandpa.

"I'll show them," she said. "I'll just do it by myself."

Liza got a pencil and some paper. She

crawled back into bed and began to write out the alphabet. She had gotten about halfway through when she stopped. The pencil dropped from her hand.

The next thing Liza knew, it was morning.

"What is my lamp doing on?" she said. She reached over to turn it off. Then she saw the paper and pencil on the floor. And she remembered why the light was on.

"Oh, phooey!" she said. "And I had it all planned out. Why did I have to fall asleep?"

All Twenty-six

Liza quickly dressed and ran downstairs. She was surprised to see only Gran and Grandpa in the kitchen.

"Where are the boys?" she asked.

"They haven't come down yet," said Grandpa. "You're the early bird today."

"Good," said Liza. "I think I just want cereal, Gran."

"Nonsense," said Gran. "You need a real breakfast."

Liza didn't argue. That bacon did smell good.

"Here you are," said Gran. "The toast will be ready in a minute."

Liza had just begun to eat when the boys came in.

"Hi," said Bill, "I'm starved."

"That's nothing unusual," said Liza. She finished her breakfast and excused herself.

"I'll be in my room," she called to the boys.

Liza went to her room. She got out a pencil and a fresh sheet of paper. On the paper Liza wrote all the letters of the alphabet. Above each letter she put a number.

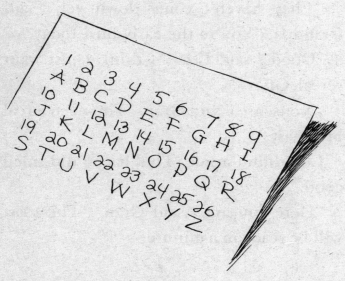

"Now, let's see," said Liza. She crossed her fingers. "Oh, this has got to work. And I've got to find out before the boys get here."

But she didn't. The boys came in just then.

"Hey, what's this?" asked Bill. "Don't you know the alphabet yet?"

"I think it's the clue to that message," said Liza.

"What do you mean?" asked Jed.

" 'All twenty-six'—the alphabet," said Liza. "The alphabet has twenty-six letters in it."

"Gee, I never thought of that," said Bill. "Where's that piece of paper?"

"Right here," said Jed.

"What's the first number on it?" asked Bill.

"Four," said Jed.

"Four—that's 'd,'" said Liza. "What's next?"

"Five and another five," said Jed.

"D-e-e. Go on," said Liza.

"Sixteen," said Jed.

"D-e-e-p," said Liza. "Deep."

"Hey, it works!" shouted Bill. "When did you figure this out?"

"In the middle of the night," said Liza.

"Why didn't you tell us?" said Bill. "We could have had this finished."

"Tell you! Are you kidding?" said Liza. "I tried my best. But neither one of you would wake up."

"So let's get it done now," said Jed. "I'll call out the numbers."

"I'll find the letters," said Liza, "and you write them down, Bill."

The children worked quickly. Soon they had figured out all of the words.

"Okay, read the whole thing, Bill," said Jed.

Bill read: " 'Deep in the woods runs a stream. On one bank is a stone. A wishing stone where you sit and dream. Find the highest side and dig.' "

"The wishing stone!" said Jed. "Do you think that's our wishing stone?"

"Unless there are two of them," said Bill.

"But it's not deep in the woods," said Liza. "Maybe there is another one."

"Let's ask Grandpa," said Jed. "He'll know about it. But remember, this is our secret."

The children raced downstairs and out the back door.

"Grandpa," they called.

"Here, out here in the barn," answered Grandpa.

The three raced out to the barn.

"My goodness, you are in a hurry," said Grandpa. "Take it easy. You'll have Mickey kicking over the bucket."

"Sorry, Grandpa," said Jed. "We didn't know you were milking."

"Now, what can I do for you?" asked Grandpa.

"We were just wondering," said Liza, "are there two wishing stones?"

"Two wishing stones!" said Grandpa. "Not that I know of. What's the matter with one? Don't tell me you have too many wishes for one stone to take care of. That stone has been hearing wishes for many a year now.''

"Was the stream ever deep in the woods?" asked Jed.

"This whole place was deep in the woods at one time," said Grandpa. "Every bit of this land had to be cleared. The lumber for the house was a part of the woods. But why did you think about all that?"

"We were just wondering," said Jed.

"Thanks, Grandpa," said Bill. "Is it all right if we go exploring?"

"Go right ahead," said Grandpa. "But you had better let Gran know you're gone."

"All right," said Liza.

The children left the barn.

"Well, that answers that question," said Jed. "Liza, you go tell Gran. Bill and I will get some shovels."

"All right," said Liza. "Do you have the message?"

"We don't need that," said Bill. "We know what it says."

"Better get the alphabet code though," said Jed. "We may need that."

Liza went to the house to tell Gran and get the code.

"Now be careful," said Gran, "and come back in time for lunch."

"We will," said Liza. "You know Bill would never be late for that."

At the Wishing Stone

Bill and Jed were waiting for Liza.

"We could only find two shovels," said Jed, "so we'll have to take turns."

"Did you bring the code?" asked Bill.

"Yes," said Liza, "I've got it."

"Then let's go," said Jed.

The children walked across the fields toward the woods.

"It would be shorter if we cut across the pasture," said Jed. "I don't see the cows. They must be in the other field."

"Okay," said Bill, "let's cut."

The three climbed the fence and started across the pasture. Soon they came to the

other side. Again they climbed the fence.

"Well, there it is," said Jed, "the wishing stone."

Liza ran to the stone and climbed up on it. She closed her eyes and made a wish.

"I bet I know what you wished," said Bill.

"Well, don't say it," said Liza, "or it won't come true."

But something else had caught Bill's eye.

"Look at that plum tree," he said. "Come on."

"No," said Jed. "We've got work to do. Can't you think of anything besides your stomach?"

"Aw, have a heart," said Bill. "I need

those plums for energy. That was a long walk. Besides, we only have two shovels. You and Liza can begin."

Jed sighed. "Oh, well, come on, Liza. He's hopeless."

Liza looked at the plums. She wouldn't admit it, but she would have liked to join Bill herself. But instead she took the shovel Jed handed her.

"I sure am glad Grandpa's grandfather told us where to dig," said Jed.

"Grandpa's grandfather—what does that make him to us?" asked Liza.

"Let me think," said Jed. "That would make him Dad's great-grandfather and our great-great-grandfather."

"Great-great-grandfather. It's easier to say Grandpa's grandfather," said Liza. "Can you tell which side is the highest?"

"Sure," said Jed. "See how it humps up over here?"

He and Liza began to dig. Liza looked over at Bill. He was stuffing plums into his mouth as fast as he could pick them. Jed and Liza dug in silence for a long time.

"How deep did he bury that thing anyway?" asked Liza. "We've already dug along this whole side."

"Can't help it," said Jed. "We have to keep going until we find it."

"Well, I'm getting tired," said Liza.

"Stop awhile," said Jed. "Maybe Bill will take his turn."

"Fat chance of that until he eats all the plums he wants," said Liza. "I'll dig awhile longer."

But soon Liza's arms gave out. She sat down.

"Hey, Bill," called Jed, "leave a few plums for us. How about taking a turn at digging?"

"Okay, okay," said Bill. He took Liza's shovel and began to work.

Liza sat on the pile of earth they had shoveled out. The damp softness of it felt good. She picked some up and let it sift through her fingers. Then she stuck her whole arm into it. Her hand hit something hard. She pulled it out of the earth. Liza thought at first that it was a rock. Then she noticed its odd shape. She brushed away the dirt around it.

"The little pot," she whispered. Then she shouted, "Hey, fellows! Look! This is it!"

"The little pot," said Jed, "the little pot that is in the picture."

"Gee," said Bill, "we didn't even notice when we dug it up. We could have dug all day."

Jed took the little pot. He tried to take the top off. But he couldn't make it budge.

"I'll have to break it," he said.

"Oh, no!" said Liza. "Can't you get it off some way? It's such a cute little pot."

"Ah, girls!" said Bill. "Go ahead and break it, Jed."

"No, Liza's right," said Jed. "If we can, we should keep it. Maybe if I had something sharp I could pry the top off."

"Let's take it back to the house," said Liza.

"It's time to go anyway," said Bill. "Gran is probably looking for us for lunch."

"Lunch!" said Jed.

"Oh, Bill," said Liza, "how did I ever get you for a twin?"

Bill made a face at Liza, grabbed a shovel, and started off.

"Here, Liza," said Jed, "you take the pot. I'll carry the other shovel."

A Pocketful of Plums

Liza took the little pot. She started after her brothers. Then she stopped. Liza looked back at the plum tree. Her mouth was watering for just one plum. Quickly she turned and ran back to the tree. She popped a fat, red plum into her mouth. How good it was! One plum led to another and Liza just couldn't stop eating them.

The boys climbed the fence and started across the field.

"Hey," said Jed, "where's Liza?"

"Liza? I thought she was right behind us," said Bill.

"Liza!" called Jed and Bill together

very loud. "Where are you? We're going!"

Liza jumped when she heard the boys. She had meant to catch up with them before they missed her.

"Coming," she called. "Go ahead. I'll catch up with you."

"Well hurry up," called Bill.

Liza stayed long enough to pick a pocketful of plums. Then she started after the boys.

The boys were almost across the pasture when Liza caught up with them.

"So what took you so long?" asked Bill.

But before Liza could answer, a big gray goose darted out of the bushes alongside them.

"Old Honker!" shouted Jed. "Run! He'll pinch like anything if he catches you."

The three children started running across the pasture. Old Honker came after them, hissing and honking at every step.

Bill made it to the fence first. He threw

his shovel across and then clambered over himself. Liza was right behind him. Jed was almost at the fence when his foot caught on a root. He fell sprawling to the ground. Before he could get up, Old Honker had him by the seat of the pants.

"Help!" called Jed. "Do something!"

Liza and Bill were too startled to move at first.

"We've got to do something quick," said Bill.

"But what?" asked Liza.

"I could throw this shovel at him," said Bill.

"No!" said Liza. "You might hit Jed."

Suddenly Liza remembered the plums. She took out a handful. Liza threw a plum

at Old Honker. It hit him on the head and bounced off. Old Honker turned his head to see what it was. The redness of the plum caught his eye. He let Jed loose and went after the plum. Liza threw another one a little farther away. Old Honker ran after that one. Jed grabbed his shovel and quickly climbed the fence while Liza kept Old Honker busy running after plums.

"That was quick thinking," said Jed. "Thanks, Liza."

"Are you all right?" asked Liza.

"Yes," said Jed. "Old Honker got in a few good pinches, but mostly he had my pants."

"Boy, I'm glad that doesn't happen every day," said Bill. "That really shook me up."

Jed chuckled. "It sure did. I never saw you move so fast."

"It was those plums," said Bill. "I knew I was going to need that extra energy."

The Second Clue

When the children reached the house, the boys put the shovels away. Then they all went inside.

"Gran," called Bill, "we're back. Is it time for lunch?"

"Lunch!" said Gran. "My, no! It's a long time before lunch."

"Oooh," groaned Bill, "how will I ever make it?"

"There's plenty of fruit," said Gran. "Help yourself."

Bill grabbed an apple.

"This might hold me for a little while," he said.

The children headed upstairs.

"We need something sharp to pry this open," said Jed.

"I've got a fingernail file," said Liza.

"That should be just the thing," said Jed.

They went into Liza's room. She got the fingernail file and handed it to Jed. Jed tried to pry the top off of the little pot. But the top would not budge.

"Give me a shoe," said Jed. "Maybe I can hammer the file in a bit and loosen it up."

Liza got one of her shoes that had a hard heel. Jed turned the little pot on its side. He put the nail file in place where the top fit onto the pot. With the shoe, he pounded on the file.

"Gee," he said, "this is going to be slow work."

Jed turned the pot a little and pounded on the file again. Bill began to get fidgety. Finally he could stand it no longer.

"Here, give it to me," he said. And before Jed could stop him, Bill grabbed the pot and the shoe. He whacked the pot as hard as he could. The little pot fell into lots of little pieces.

"That takes care of that," he said.

Liza and Jed were horrified.

"Oh, Bill!" cried Liza, "how could you?"

"You really didn't have to do that," said Jed.

"So who cares about a little old pot," said Bill.

"I do," shouted Liza. "You're just hateful."

"Well, we can't do anything about it now," said Jed, "but somebody better clean up this mess before Gran finds it."

Liza glared at Bill.

"All right, all right," said Bill, "I'll clean it up."

The children looked down at the broken pieces of pottery. Right in the middle was a leather pouch. Jed picked up the pouch.

"Bill made me so mad," said Liza, "I almost forgot about the clue."

"I guess it's inside of this pouch," said Jed. "Grandpa's grandfather sure wasn't taking any chances with it."

"Hurry and open it," said Liza.

Jed pulled the pouch apart. He took out a folded piece of paper.

"Oh, oh," he said, "this is just as brittle as the first one was."

"I've got the paste and paper ready," said Liza.

Liza spread paste on the paper. Jed carefully unfolded the paper. At each fold the paper broke.

"Hey, that's pretty good," he said. "Only four pieces this time."

"Hurry up, Liza," said Bill, "I've got the code ready."

"Stop being so bossy," said Liza. "I'm hurrying as fast as I can."

Liza pasted on the last piece.

"And besides that," she said, "I don't think you need that code."

"You mean Grandpa's grandfather just wrote out what he had to say?" asked Jed.

"No," said Liza, "but it's not the same kind of puzzle. See if you can figure it out."

Jed took the paper. He read, " '1 2 14 is a kind of monkey. 5 6 3 20 is a fruit. 27 7 13 19 means to eat dinner. 64 28 41 42 12 39 is a color. 11 15 22 8 56 34 is the same as throws. 9 54 4 58 63 is an animal to ride. 35 21 24 is something to play with. 17 50 26 47 62 means to use your head. 43 33 38 30 is meat from a steer. 48 57 10 60 is something to eat from. 18 46 25 52 is the sound an angry goose makes. 55 40 23 59 is a bird's home. 31 61 16 is a number. 32 36 53 is the opposite of cold. 37 29 49 51 is a short letter. 45 44 is the opposite of she.' "

"Is that supposed to mean something?" asked Bill. "Grandpa's grandfather—hey, what does that make him to us?"

"Our great-great-grandfather!" shouted Liza and Jed.

"Well, you don't have to bite my head off," said Bill. "I just asked."

"We figured it out this morning," said Jed. "I wish this thing was as easy to figure out. Anybody have any ideas?"

The children studied the paper for awhile.

"Wait a minute," said Liza. "I think I know what to do. What's the highest number?"

Jed looked through the numbers.

"Sixty-four," he said.

Liza took a fresh sheet of paper. She began writing numbers.

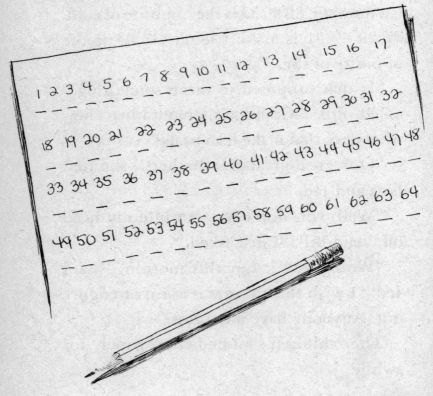

"Oh, I see what you're doing," said Jed.

"Well, I don't," said Bill.

"Just a minute and you will," said Liza. " '1 2 14 is a kind of monkey.' "

" 'Ape,' " said Jed.

Liza wrote "a" under 1, "p" under 2, and "e" under 14.

"Oh, now I see," said Bill. "I hope you're right."

" '5 6 3 20 is a fruit,' " read Liza.

" 'Pear,' " said Bill.

" 'Means to eat dinner,' " said Liza.

" 'Dine,' " said Jed. "Gee, this is fun."

" 'Is a color'—six letters," said Liza. "P-u-r-p-l-e—I'll bet that's it."

Liza wrote the letters under the proper numbers.

"What's next?" asked Bill.

" 'Is the same as throws,' " said Liza.

" 'Tosses,' " said Bill. "Does that fit?"

Liza counted the letters in "tosses."

"Yes," she said. "It has six letters and that's what we need. The next is 'an animal to ride.' I know that must be 'horse.' "

"You write too slowly," said Bill. "Here, let me do some."

"All right," said Liza. "The next one is 'something to play with.' "

" 'Toy,' " said Bill, and he quickly wrote it in.

" 'Means to use your head,' " said Liza. "Boy, we're sure having to do that now."

"So what's the word?" asked Bill.

" 'Think,' " shouted Jed and Liza.

"Oh, stop fooling around and tell me the word if you know it," said Bill.

" 'Think'—t-h-i-n-k, that's the word," said Jed.

"Boy," said Bill, "how dumb can I be!"

" 'Is meat from a steer,' " said Liza. "And that's 'pork.' "

82

"So let's take the highest," said Bill. He filled in the letters for "ten."

" 'The opposite of cold,' " said Liza. "That one has to be 'hot.' But this next one is funny—'a short letter.' "

"Short letter," said Bill. "Lots of letters are short, but how do you spell them?"

"You're both nuts," said Jed. "I think this means the kind of letter you get in the mail."

"Well, I still don't know the answer," said Liza.

" 'Note!' " said Bill. "Now who's so dumb?"

"Sorry," said Jed. "The last one is 'the opposite of she' and that has to be 'he.' "

"How does the whole thing look?" asked Liza.

The three children crowded around the paper.

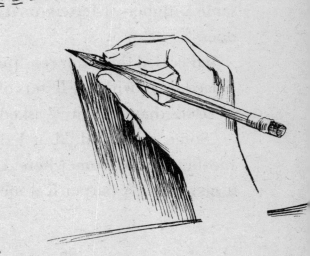

1 2 3 4 5 6 7 8 9 10 11 12 13 14 15 16 17
A P A R P E I S # S I L N E O N I

18 19 20 21 22 23 24 25 26 27 28 29 30 31 32
H E R O S S Y S I D U O F T H

33 34 35 36 37 38 39 40 41 42 43 44 45 46 47 48
E S T O N E E R P B E H I N D

49 50 51 52 53 54 55 56 57 58 59 60 61 62 63 64
T H E S T O N E I S T H E K E P

"Doesn't look like anything but a bunch of gibberish to me," said Bill. "Anybody have another idea to try?"

"Wait," said Jed. "Look at that last line. See, it says, 'the stone is the kep.' I'll bet that's supposed to be 'key.'"

"What word is number 64 in?" asked Bill. "Let me see that paper a minute. Here it is. The first letter in the name of a color. It should begin with 'y' instead of 'p.' What color begins with a 'y'?"

"'Yellow,'" said Liza. "And it has the same number of letters in it that 'purple' does."

Jed erased the letters of "purple" and replaced them with the letters of "yellow."

"Does that help any?" asked Bill.

"Some," said Jed, "but I think we have another mistake somewhere. Listen to what it says now. 'A parpeish stone on the rossy side of the stone well behind the stone is the key.' "

" 'A parpeish stone on the rossy side'? That really sounds cuckoo," said Bill.

"Give it to me a minute," said Liza. " 'Parpeish'—I'll bet that's supposed to be purplish. Let me find 3. Yes, here it is. 'The name of a fruit.' What fruit has a 'u' in it?"

The children thought a minute.

" 'Plum'!" said Bill. "We should have thought of that first thing after this morning. Take out 'pear.' "

Liza quickly changed the letters.

"There," she said. " 'A purplish stone on the mossy side of the stone well. Behind the stone is the key.' "

"Hooray! We did it!" shouted Bill. Then he stopped.

"What's the matter?" asked Jed.

"What stone well?" asked Bill.

"That's what I would like to know," said Liza. They both turned to Jed.

"You know," said Jed, "there's only one around here. It's out back."

Bill and Liza still looked puzzled.

"Where Gran has flowers planted," said Jed.

"Gran's petunia bed?" said Liza. "That's not a well."

"Not now," said Jed. "Grandpa had it filled in a long time ago. He said it wasn't used, and open wells are dangerous."

"Yipee!" shouted Bill. "All out for Gran's petunia well."

"Let's hope Gran doesn't see us," said Jed. "She loves those petunias."

The Key

The three ran downstairs and out the back door. In just a minute they were standing around the stone well.

" 'The mossy side of the stone well,' " said Liza. "I like the way that sounds."

Bill walked all around the well.

"There's just one problem," he said, "there is no mossy side."

The children stared at each other. Bill was right. There was no moss on the well.

Jed scratched his head.

"Watch out!" said Bill. "Jed's thinking."

Bill and Liza looked at Jed.

"Of course!" said Jed. "There's no water

in the well. Moss only grows where it's damp.''

"That's a big help," said Bill. "I suppose we have to take the whole well apart."

"Now just a minute," said Jed. "Moss would also only grow where there is shade."

"So that helps, too," said Bill. "Where is there any shade around this well?"

The three children sat down to think this through.

Suddenly Liza jumped up.

"Gosh, we are stupid!" she said.

"What! What!" said Bill.

"Shade," said Liza. "Look what we're sitting on."

Bill and Jed looked down.

"A tree stump!" said Jed. "For gosh sakes. We sure are stupid. I remember Grandpa just had it cut down a couple of years ago."

"So we're stupid," said Bill. "Let's find that purplish stone."

They looked at each stone on the side of the well facing the stump.

"Purplish stone! Phooey," said Bill. "Do you think maybe our great-great-grandfather was color blind?"

"Don't even think such things!" said Liza. "We may be taking the well apart sure enough."

"Hey, this stone looks different," said

91

"Uh-uh," said Bill. "Even I know that. Pork comes from a pig. Beef comes from a steer."

"Okay," said Liza, "so we're even now. Next?"

" 'Is something to eat from,' " said Jed.

" 'Plate,' " said Liza.

"Nope," said Bill, "only four letters."

" 'Dish,' " said Jed.

"Okay," said Bill, "next?"

" 'Is the sound an angry goose makes,' " said Liza.

" 'Hiss,' " Jed laughed. "I sure should know that!"

" 'A bird's home,' " said Liza. "That's easy, 'nest.' "

" 'A number,' " said Jed. "Gee, it has only three letters."

"Could be 'one,' " said Liza.

"Or 'two,' or 'ten,' " said Jed.

Jed. "I guess it could be called purplish."

Bill and Liza looked at the stone.

"That's not my idea of purplish," said Liza, "but it's the nearest we've come to it. Maybe you're right."

"Let's try to get it out," said Bill. "That's the only way to tell."

"Somebody get a file out of the toolbox," said Jed. "We'll need something sharp to pry it out."

"Okay," said Bill. He ran toward the tool-shed.

Jed took a stick and began digging around the stone.

Bill ran back with the file.

"Here," he said. "Is the stone loose?"

"I can't tell yet," said Jed.

Jed worked carefully. He went around the outside of the stone with the file. Dirt fell out as he dug.

"I need a hammer," he said.

Without a word Liza ran to the toolshed. She came back with a hammer and handed it to Jed.

"If that's the one," said Bill, "why is it so hard to get out?"

"Oh, come on, Bill," said Jed, "that stone has been in place for over a hundred years. Do you expect it to fall out just because we're here?"

"I sure wish it would," said Bill.

Jed took the hammer. He placed the point of the file in the little ridge he had dug out around the stone. He gave the end of the file several sharp blows. The stone moved.

"Okay," said Jed, "it's loosening up now."

Jed pried at the stone again and again with the file.

"Here it comes!" he shouted.

The stone fell out, rolled over on the ground, and came to a halt.

Quickly Jed stuck his hand into the hole. Bill and Liza held their breath.

"There's something there all right," said Jed, "but it's wedged in. Maybe I can get it with the file."

Jed poked around in the hole with the file. Then he reached in and pulled out a small object. It was covered with green mold.

"Ugh," said Liza, "that looks terrible."

"It feels terrible, too," said Jed dropping the object on the grass. He quickly wiped his hands on his pants.

"Oh, look at your pants," said Liza. "If Gran sees that!"

Jed looked at his pants. There were green smudges where he had wiped his hands.

"Yeah, if Gran saw that she would know we were up to something," said Jed. "Does anybody have anything I can wipe them off with?"

"Here," said Liza, "I'll do it with this tissue."

Liza cleaned the pants as best she could. Then she took another tissue and began to clean off the package Jed dropped.

"It's a leather pouch again," said Jed. "Gosh, if there's a note in this, it's probably spoiled."

"I can't wait to see if the key is really there," said Liza.

Jed pulled at the leather pouch, but it was stuck tight.

"It's sealed itself together," said Jed. He

took the file and began to pry the leather apart. Finally he had a hole big enough to stick his fingers into.

"Is it there?" asked Bill.

"Yes!" said Jed. He reached in and pulled out a strange-looking key.

"It looks just like the key in the picture," whispered Liza. "The key to the treasure!"

"Of course it does, silly," said Bill. "Great-great-grandfather wouldn't hide one key and make a picture of another one. Say, Jed, is there another piece of paper?"

"Yes," said Jed, "I'm trying to get it out now."

"Oh, do you really think it's spoiled?" asked Liza. "I just couldn't bear it if we got this close to finding the treasure and something happened."

"I don't think you have to worry," said Jed. "This pouch is just as dry as can be inside. Now if I can just get the paper out without tearing it to bits."

Jed took the file and ripped a larger opening in the pouch. Carefully he drew out a folded piece of paper.

"Yipee! Success!" he shouted and waved the paper in the air.

"Let's go find out what it says," said Bill.

"Children," called Gran, "come and wash up for lunch."

A Difficult Lunchtime

"Oh, bother," said Liza. "I don't want lunch now."

"This is one time," said Bill, "that not even I am ready for lunch."

"Well, we can't tell Gran that," said Jed. "Let's just try to get through quickly."

The children went into the house and upstairs to wash. Liza put the key and the paper on her bed. Then they all went down for lunch.

Liza played around with the food on her plate. She felt so excited inside that she couldn't swallow a bite. Bill was eating, but he was bouncing up and down on his chair the whole time. And Jed seemed unable to get comfortable any way he sat. But not one of the three talked. They had decided that lunch would get over quicker if they just concentrated on eating.

"I declare," said Grandpa, "I never saw you this quiet before. And Liza hasn't touched her food."

"It's no wonder," said Gran. "They must be worn out, the way they've been rushing around all morning."

"Well, just slow down a bit," said Grandpa. "You've got all summer."

Liza could keep quiet no longer. She said, "But we're having such fun. You'll never guess what we found!"

Jed began shaking his head at Liza. But Bill was closer to her. He lifted his foot under the table and gave Liza a sharp kick.

"Ouch!" said Liza. "You stop kicking me, Bill. I want to tell Gran about the plum tree."

"Sorry," said Bill, "I thought you were going to tell about—"

"The goose!" interrupted Jed quickly.

Bill turned red and stammered, "That's right, the goose."

"The goose!" said Grandpa. "What about the goose?"

Jed started to tell them about his adventure with Old Honker.

Liza looked at Bill and they both started to giggle. Liza put her hand over her mouth

and tried to stop. But the giggles kept coming. Jed did his best to keep a straight face, but he couldn't. Soon he was giggling, too.

Grandpa said, "If it was that funny, tell us, too. Gran and I like a good laugh."

This made the children giggle harder. They couldn't say a thing. Finally Gran said, "All right, that's enough. Remember you are at the table."

The children looked down at their plates. They knew from Gran's tone of voice that she was annoyed with them. Everything was quiet for a minute. Then Liza happened to look at Bill just as he took a big swallow of milk. They just couldn't help it. They had to giggle. And Bill spouted milk all over the table.

There was complete silence in the room.

"Gee, Gran, I-I'm sorry," stammered Bill, "I-I'll clean it up."

Bill got some paper towels and began to clean up the mess. Liza went around and helped him. Gran didn't say a word about the incident.

Suddenly there was a loud noise outside. Everybody jumped.

"What's that?" asked Liza.

"Mr. Sanders and his buzz saw," said Grandpa. "He is going to clear out that limb in the big oak. He'll also put up the rope for you."

"Oh boy," said Bill. "How long will it take him?"

"He should finish this afternoon," said Grandpa. "It depends on how much trouble he has getting that limb down."

"There's Mrs. Sanders and Timothy," said Gran. "She said they might visit while

Mr. Sanders was working in the yard."

Gran got up from the table. She went to the back door. A woman and small boy were in the yard.

"Do come in," called Gran.

"I saw you were having lunch," said Mrs. Sanders. "Go ahead and finish. We'll wait out here."

"Nonsense," said Gran, "come on in. We were just getting up."

Grandpa left the table, too.

Bill motioned to Jed and Liza.

"Gosh," he said, "suppose Gran asks us to look after Timothy."

Jed groaned. "She just couldn't do that to us. Or could she?"

"After what happened at lunch, we sure couldn't say no if she did," said Bill.

"Wait a minute," said Liza. "I've got an idea that I'm sure will work."

"What is it?" asked Jed.

"Shh," said Liza, "here's Grandpa."

Grandpa got his hat and said, "I better go out and see if I can help Mr. Sanders."

Grandpa held the door open. Mrs. Sanders and Timothy came in.

"Welcome, welcome," said Grandpa. "Hi there, Timothy."

"Hi," said Timothy.

Liza started to clear the table. She said, "Gee, Gran, we're awfully tired. After we wash the dishes, do you think we should rest?"

"That's a very sensible idea," said Gran. "And I'll do the dishes. It won't take me but a few minutes. Mrs. Sanders will talk to me and Timothy loves to play with the pots and pans. Don't you, Timothy?"

"Yep," said Timothy. He went straight to the cabinet where Gran kept the pots and pans. He opened the door and began to take them out.

"You remember my grandchildren, don't you?" Gran asked Mrs. Sanders.

"Indeed I do," said Mrs. Sanders. "I've known them since they were as young as Timothy. How are you?"

"Fine, thank you," said Liza.

"Now run along," said Gran. She turned to Mrs. Sanders. "They've just worn themselves out trying to do everything at once."

The Third Clue

The children quickly went upstairs to Liza's room.

"That was a good idea, Liza," said Jed, "but how did you know it would work?"

"Because grown-ups are always wanting children to rest," said Liza.

Liza held up the strange-looking key and looked at it.

"This key makes me feel all creepy inside," she said.

"I know what you mean," said Jed. "It just doesn't seem real."

"Well, it is," said Bill. "Let's get on with this and see what Great-great-grandfather is telling us to do now."

"That's the thing about it," said Liza, "our great-great-grandfather *is* telling us what to do."

"I wonder what he would say about that," said Jed.

"Probably tell us to quit fooling around and get to work," said Bill.

Jed and Liza laughed.

"So let's do just that," said Jed. He carefully unfolded the paper, but as before, the paper broke at every fold.

"I've got the paste ready," said Liza. She quickly pasted the pieces onto a sheet of paper.

"A crossword puzzle!" she exclaimed.

"Crossword puzzle!" said Jed. "I didn't even know they had them in those days."

"Maybe they didn't," said Bill. "Maybe Great-great-grandfather invented them."

"He sure invented this one," said Jed. "I never saw one numbered this way."

The children studied the puzzle.

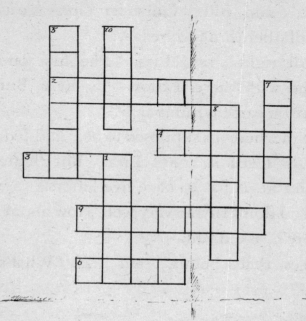

1. Rhymes with there
2. Purple flowers
3. What seeds do when planted
4. Comes before fourth
5. Helps support a house
6. The opposite of right
7. Rhymes with wide
8. The center
9. A hole for a key
10. The opposite of push

"Roll up your sleeves and let's get to work," said Bill. "Can't let Great-great-grandfather think we're lazy."

"All right," said Liza. "The first one rhymes with 'there.' I know—it's, 'here.' But where on earth is number 1?"

"Not where it's supposed to be," said Jed.

"Oh, I see it," said Liza. "But 'here' doesn't fit. It has to have five letters."

"You don't rhyme very well. How about, 'where'?" asked Bill.

"Yes, that's better," said Liza. "What's next?"

" 'Purple flowers,' " said Jed.

"That man sure liked purple," said Bill. "Purplish stone, purple flowers. Does 'roses' fit?"

"Roses!" said Liza. "Roses aren't purple."

" 'Lilacs'!" said Jed.

"Of course," said Liza.

" 'What seeds do when planted,' " read Jed.

" 'Grow,' " said Bill. "What's next?"

" 'Comes before fourth,' " said Jed.

" 'Fifth,' " said Bill.

"Jeepers," said Jed, "Great-great-grandfather would either laugh or groan if he could hear that."

"Now what did I do?" asked Bill.

"Said fifth comes before fourth," said Jed.

"Oh, before—I didn't hear that," said Bill. "It's 'third.' "

" 'Helps support a house,' " read Jed.

"You've got me there," said Bill.

" 'Frame'?" asked Liza.

"Nope, that has only five letters. This word has six," said Jed.

The children sat and stared at the paper.

"Oh, I know! 'Pillar,' " said Liza. "But I'm not sure how to spell it."

"P-i-l-l-o-w," said Jed, "that's six letters."

"Uh-uh," said Bill, "that's a different word."

"Bill's right," said Liza, "it has to end in 'r.' "

"It's p-i-l-l-a-r," said Bill.

"Congratulations," said Jed. "Now—'the opposite of right.' That must be 'wrong.' "

"Too many letters," said Liza. "What else is the opposite of 'right'?"

" 'Left,' " said Bill.

"Hey, you're getting pretty sharp," said Jed.

"Just took me a little time to warm up," said Bill.

"Okay, here's the next one," said Jed. " 'Rhymes with wide.' "

" 'Tide,' 'hide,' 'side,' " said Bill, "take your pick."

"I'll vote for 'hide,' " said Liza, and she wrote it into the puzzle.

"How many more of these things are there?" asked Bill.

"Only three," said Jed. "The next one is 'the center.' That should be 'middle.' "

"And 'middle' fits," said Liza.

" 'A hole for a key,' " read Jed.

"That's a silly one," said Bill.

"So what's the word?" asked Liza.

" 'Keyhole,' " said Bill.

"Phooey," said Liza, "I should have known that."

"And the last one is 'the opposite of push,' " said Jed.

" 'Pull,' " said Liza and Bill together.

"Well, the puzzle is finished," said Jed. "I wonder what we do now?"

The children looked at the finished puzzle. And they were completely baffled. There was no clue as to what to do next.

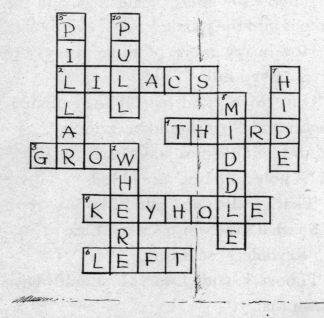

1. Rhymes with there
2. Purple flowers
6. The opposite of right
7. Rhymes with wide

Suddenly Bill jumped up.

"The numbers!" he said.

"What about the numbers?" asked Jed.

"Maybe we're supposed to arrange the words in the order of the numbers," said Bill. "Here, I'll show you what I mean."

Bill took another sheet of paper.

"See, number 1 is 'where,' number 2 is 'lilacs,' and number 3 is 'grow,' " said Bill. "Do you get it? 'Where lilacs grow.' "

"That makes sense," said Jed. "Go ahead."

Bill quickly copied the words in order, according to their numbers.

"Hey!" said Jed. "We didn't have to do the puzzle after all. We could have just solved the clues."

"Great-great-grandfather just wanted to mix us up a little!" said Bill.

"Oh, hurry and read it," said Liza.

"Here goes," said Bill. " 'Where lilacs grow third pillar left hide——' "

"Whoa, boy," said Jed, "I think we made a mistake there. Try 'side' instead of 'hide.' "

"Okay," said Bill. " 'Where lilacs grow third pillar left side middle keyhole pull.' "

"That doesn't make much sense to me," said Liza.

"Sure it does," said Jed. "You know where the lilacs grow by the side of the house. In the third pillar in the middle of the left side there should be a keyhole. We're supposed to put the key in it and pull."

"Well, it didn't sound that simple," said Liza.

"I'm not sure that is what it means," said Bill. "Those lilac bushes couldn't have lived that long."

"No," said Liza, "but don't you remember Grandpa told us how Great-great-grand-father planted lilac bushes as soon as the house was built. And ever since that time, there have been lilac bushes on that side of the house."

"Hey," said Jed. "The third pillar! That's behind the bush we use for our hide-out. All these years we've been playing right next to the treasure."

Trouble All Around

Liza grabbed up the key and ran downstairs. Jed and Bill followed her. Liza was the first to reach the lilac bushes.

"You're right," she called, "it is our hideout."

Liza plunged into the bushes. And she plunged out even faster screaming, "Wasps —a wasp stung me!"

"Where? Where?" asked Jed. "Let me see."

"Here, on my arm," said Liza hopping from one foot to the other. Her eyes filled with tears.

"Ooh, it hurts! It hurts!" she cried and

held out her arm for the boys to see. There was a red circle beginning to swell.

"Better go to Gran," said Bill.

Liza ran into the house.

"Let's see where the nest is," said Jed. He and Bill got on their hands and knees and looked under the bush.

"I see it," said Bill.

"Where?" asked Jed. "Oh, yes, I see it, too."

There, hanging on the underside of one of the lilac branches, was a gray, papery-looking wasps' nest. Wasps were milling all around it.

"Gee, it sure is a big one," said Jed. "There must be a hundred wasps there."

But Bill was looking at something else now. He picked up a stick.

"Hey, are you crazy or something?" said Jed. "If you go fooling around that nest with a stick, you're going to get stung, too."

"Don't worry," said Bill, "I'm not going to tangle with any wasps. But Liza dropped the key."

Quietly Bill reached under the bush with the stick. Slowly he dragged the key out. Then he and Jed went in to see about Liza.

Liza was holding an ice cube to her arm. Bill slipped through the kitchen, went upstairs, and put the key away. He came down just as Grandpa came in. Grandpa saw Liza with the ice cube.

"What happened to you?" he asked.

"A wasp stung me," said Liza.

"Wasp!" said Grandpa. "I didn't know there was a nest around. Come on, boys, show me where you were."

Jed and Bill took Grandpa around to the lilac bushes.

"You'll have to get down on your knees to see it, Grandpa," said Jed.

Grandpa knelt down and Jed pointed to the nest.

"It's a big one all right," said Grandpa. "Liza was lucky only one stung her. And it's right where you children liked to play last summer. Well, there's nothing we can do about it until dusk. We'll have to wait until they settle down for the night. Then we can burn them out."

They all went back inside. Liza and Timothy were sitting at the kitchen table having lemonade and cookies. The boys told Liza what Grandpa had said. Then they, too, had lemonade and cookies.

Gran and Mrs. Sanders came into the kitchen. Timothy climbed down from his chair.

"Mrs. Sanders," said Liza, "would you like for us to take Timothy outside for a while?"

"That's nice of you to offer," said Mrs. Sanders, "but Timothy doesn't like the noise of the buzz saw. He'll be all right in here."

The three children went outside.

"Did you really want to baby-sit?" asked Bill.

"Well, there's nothing else to do," said Liza.

"I'd rather do nothing than that," said Bill.

Liza kicked at the dirt and said, "Oh, why did this have to happen! We were so close to the treasure. Now we'll have to wait until tomorrow."

"Stupid old wasps," said Bill. "With all the bushes around this place, they had to pick that one."

Bill picked up a rock and threw it.

"Hey, look what you're doing," shouted Jed. "You almost hit me with that rock."

"Sorry," mumbled Bill.

The children wandered out toward the old oak.

"Don't come any closer," called Mr. Sanders. "This limb is too big to pull down. We're having to saw it out in pieces. Can't

tell where the pieces will land. I don't want any of you getting clomped on the head."

"All right, Mr. Sanders," said Bill, "we'll stay back."

The children watched from where they were for a while. But soon they got bored with that, too. They wandered all over the place. Never had an afternoon seemed so long.

Finally Mr. Sanders and his helpers began to load up the equipment in the back of Mr. Sanders' truck. Mr. Sanders called to Grandpa.

"I'll come back tomorrow and haul all of this away," he said. "I've got to get home now and feed the livestock. I had no idea this would be such a tough job."

"That will be fine," said Grandpa.

Mrs. Sanders and Timothy got into the truck with Mr. Sanders.

Mr. Sanders said, "I'll put up that rope

swing for you children tomorrow, too."

As they drove away, Timothy yelled, "Good-bye, big children, good-bye."

The children called back to him.

Still More Trouble

"Oh, Grandpa," said Liza, "is it all right to climb the tree now?"

"Yes," said Grandpa. "Mr. Sanders got the limb down."

"Let's play a game of tree tag," said Jed. "I'll be it."

The children scrambled along the low-hanging branches of the old oak. Nobody knew how old that tree was, but it was huge. Some of the branches touched the ground. They were wide enough to walk along. This was the children's favorite place to play.

Grandpa stayed and watched them. After a while he said, "I see Gran on the back porch. I think she's looking for us. Supper must be ready."

Jed and Bill ran toward the house. Liza took Grandpa's hand and skipped along beside him.

After supper Liza said, "Gee, Grandpa, isn't it dark enough yet?"

"Dark enough?" asked Grandpa.

"The wasps, Grandpa," said Bill.

"Oh, I forgot all about them," said Grandpa. "Get a flashlight and let's go."

Grandpa got some newspapers. Bill got the flashlight, and they went out.

"I have to stop by the toolshed and pick up a hoe," said Grandpa.

Bill held the light so Grandpa could see. Grandpa got the hoe and wrapped newspapers around the lower end. They went to the lilac bush.

Grandpa struck a match and lit the newspaper.

"All right," he said, "shine the light on the nest."

Bill did, and Grandpa stuck the burning paper under the wasps' nest. There was a sizzling sound. Then the nest burst into a quick bright flame. Grandpa pulled the torch away. He dropped it to the ground and stamped out the fire.

"Here, let me have that flashlight," said Grandpa. He got on his knees and looked at the place where the nest had been. Then he looked at the ground underneath.

"Just wanted to make sure none of the wasps dropped to the ground," said Grandpa, "but we seem to have burned all of them. Tomorrow you'll have your hide-out back."

All evening the children were restless. They couldn't sit still and they couldn't get interested in anything. Finally Gran put her sewing down.

"What is wrong with you children? You haven't been yourselves all day," she said.

Bill looked at Liza and Jed.

"Let's tell them," he said.

"Oh, yes, please, let's," said Liza.

Jed lifted his eyes to the picture above the mantel.

"We found the clues," he said.

"You what!" said Gran and Grandpa at once. Grandpa jumped out of his chair.

"Come on, come on," he said, "tell us where!"

Then all three of the children tried to tell the story at the same time. Finally Gran and Grandpa got it all straight.

"Well, I never," said Grandpa. "And that feathered bonnet did hold the first clue. But who would have ever thought to pull the feathers out!"

"And you were able to keep all that a secret!" said Gran. "I don't see how you did it."

"We wanted to surprise Grandpa," said Liza, and she suddenly burst into tears.

Grandpa put his arms around her and said, "Well, you certainly did, and it's the most exciting surprise I ever had."

Bill started to ask Liza why she was crying. Then he noticed Gran wiping her eyes. Suddenly he felt a lump in his throat too.

Then Grandpa said, "Say, how about letting Gran and me have a look at that key? We've sure waited long enough to see it."

"Oh, gosh," said Liza, "I think I dropped it when that wasp stung me."

"But your twin brother found it," said Bill. "I'll be right back."

Bill ran upstairs. But he did not come right back. Finally he came slowly down the stairs. He looked white.

"The key," he said. "It's gone!"

"Gone!" said everybody.

"But how?" asked Jed. "Are you sure you looked in the right place?"

Bill nodded his head. Everybody went upstairs. They searched everywhere, but no key.

"I don't understand it," said Bill. "I know I put it here on the dresser."

Nobody knew what to think about the whole situation.

Timothy

"Oh!" cried Liza, "Timothy! Gran, this afternoon when we were out, did Timothy come upstairs?"

"My, yes," said Gran. "He was all over the place. He loves to climb up and down the stairs. Oh, no! Do you think he picked up the key?"

"Let's call and see," said Liza.

Grandpa started for the phone, but Gran stopped him.

"It wouldn't do any good to call tonight," she said. "Timothy would be in bed asleep. Remember, he's not much more than a baby."

"We'll go over first thing in the morning then," said Grandpa.

The rest of the evening finally passed. Even Gran and Grandpa were restless. Nobody slept very well that night. Next morning everybody was up early.

"Hurry, Gran," said Liza, "let's go and see Timothy now."

"Goodness, Liza," said Gran, "we'll eat breakfast first. We have to give them a chance to get up too. Why don't you squeeze the orange juice for me?"

"All right," said Liza. Quickly she cut some oranges and began to squeeze them. She was just about halfway through when her arm hit the pitcher and the whole thing fell to the floor.

"Oh, no! Gran, look what happened!" said Liza.

Gran went over to help Liza get the

mess cleaned up, and the bacon burned.

Liza was almost in tears.

"Oh, Gran! Everything is going wrong," she said. "Can't we have breakfast when we come back?"

"Nonsense," said Gran. "We'll put everything right in just a few minutes."

Gran was as good as her word. Soon she had breakfast on the table. The children hadn't thought they were hungry, but the smell of the food changed their minds.

After breakfast, no one could wait any longer. They all piled in the car and started for the Sanders' house.

Mrs. Sanders and Timothy were in the yard. Mrs. Sanders was very surprised to see them.

"Pardon our coming so early," said Grandpa, "but the children lost a key. They wanted to ask Timothy if he had seen it."

"A key?" said Mrs. Sanders. "Timothy was playing with something after we came home yesterday."

Liza got out of the car and ran to Timothy.

"Timothy," she said, "did you pick up a big key yesterday?"

Timothy ran to his mother and hid his

face in her skirt. Liza followed him. Liza took a stick. Quickly she drew a picture of the key on the ground.

"See, Timothy, it looked like this," she said.

Timothy peeped around his mother's skirt. He smiled.

"Did you see a key like this?" asked Liza.

Timothy nodded his head.

"What did you do with it?" asked Liza.

"Put it in my pocket," said Timothy.

"Did you bring it home with you?" asked Liza.

Timothy nodded again.

"Is it still in your pocket?" asked Liza.

"Nope," said Timothy.

"What did you do with it?" asked Liza.

"Threw it," said Timothy.

"Threw it!" said Jed. "Where did you throw it?"

"Out there," said Timothy, pointing his finger.

"Gee, we'll never see that key again," said Jed.

"Wait, Jed," said Liza. "What happened then, Timothy?"

"Spot brought it back to me," said Timothy.

"Did you throw it again?" asked Bill.

"Yep," said Timothy, "and Spot, he brought it back to me. Spot, he's a good dog."

"Then what did you do?" asked Jed. "Did you throw it again?"

"Nope," said Timothy. "Buried it."

"Buried it!" said Liza. "Where did you bury it?"

"Sandbox," said Timothy.

"Did you dig it up again?" asked Liza.

"Nope," said Timothy.

"Is it still there?" asked Bill.

"Yep," said Timothy.

"Show us your sandbox," said Jed.

Timothy took the children to the sand-box.

"Now show us where you buried the key," said Liza.

Timothy got into the sandbox. He began to dig and make a big pile of dirt. Then he sat down and began to pat the dirt into a mound. The children waited to see what he was going to do.

"See," said Timothy, "I can make a sand castle."

"But the key, where is the key, Timothy?" asked Liza.

Timothy did not answer. He went back to building his sand castle. Bill was getting more and more angry. Finally he stepped into the sandbox and kicked Timothy's sand castle down. Timothy began to scream.

"Oh, Bill," said Jed, "why did you do that? Now he'll never tell us where the key is."

"He'll never tell anyway. I don't think he even knows," said Bill. He was very angry.

Liza went to Timothy and said, "I'll build you a great big castle, Timothy."

Timothy stopped screaming. He said, "You will?"

"Yes," said Liza, "and while I build the castle, you find the key. Okay?"

"Okay," said Timothy.

Liza piled sand and began to pat it into a castle shape. Timothy watched her, but he did not look for the key. Liza scooped up some more sand to put on the castle. Her hand hit something hard. Timothy saw what it was and grabbed it.

"Here it is, here it is," he said and held up
the key.

"Hurray," shouted Jed and Bill.

Liza took the key from Timothy and gave him a big hug.

"Oh, Timothy," she said, "you're a good boy."

"Huh," said Bill, "I can think of lots of other things to call him that would fit better."

Timothy ran to his mother shouting, "I found it! I found the key for the big children."

The Treasure

As soon as the car stopped in front of the house, the children jumped out. They ran around to the third pillar. Gran and Grandpa followed them.

"These bushes are so thick," said Jed.

"I'll fix that," said Grandpa.

He got the clippers. In a few quick whacks he had the bushes cleared from around the pillar.

Jed, Bill, and Liza crowded around the left side of the pillar. They looked it over carefully. But all that met their eyes was ordinary bricks.

"But it's got to be here," said Jed. Then

he did notice something different. "Do you see that crack?" he said.

"Hey!" said Bill. "It goes straight across the middle of the pillar."

"And look!" said Liza excitedly. "It's also cracked from the middle down to the bottom. Is there a crack like this on the other side?"

"Yes," said Jed. "It must be a door."

"But where's the keyhole?" asked Bill.

"It should be about here," said Jed. But there was no sign of a keyhole where Jed pointed.

"It kind of sinks *in* here," said Liza. "Do you think that could be it?"

"I never saw a keyhole in the middle of a door," said Bill.

"Anybody have a knife?" asked Jed.

"Here, take mine," said Grandpa.

Jed began to scrape at the place Liza had found.

"I think you're right, Liza!" he said. "This is just dirt."

Jed poked and he scraped. Finally there was an empty hole!

"The key," he said. Liza handed him the key. He put it through the hole and turned it. Jed pulled. He pulled as hard as he could, but nothing happened.

"It's stuck all the way around," he said. "Give me that knife again."

Jed worked and worked to scrape out the dirt. Liza danced all around. She just couldn't keep still. And Gran was wringing her hands in excitement.

Finally Jed said, "Help me pull, Bill."

Both boys grabbed the key. They pulled with all their might.

"Watch out!" shouted Grandpa. "Here it comes."

Jed and Bill jumped aside. A large piece from the side of the pillar tumbled to the ground.

Everyone stared at the gaping hole in the pillar.

Finally Grandpa said excitedly, "Well, isn't anybody going to find out what's in there?"

Then the children went into action. Jed

reached into the pillar and pulled out a bulky package. He handed it to Bill and pulled out another and another. He felt around inside the pillar.

"I guess that's it," he said.

"Oh, look!" said Liza. "There's a name on this package. 'Jack.'"

"My father," said Grandpa softly.

"And here's Frank's, and this one says 'Mary,'" said Bill.

The three packages lay on the ground. Everyone was quiet, staring at those packages that were meant for another set of children so many years ago. It was as though a spell had been cast. Nobody made a move to open the packages.

Then Bill broke the silence. He pounced upon the package marked "Frank." Quickly he ripped away the brittle paper and pulled out a horrible-looking mask.

"Wow!" he shouted. "This is even better than I expected."

Bill held the mask in front of his face and started dancing around, shouting war whoops.

Gran, Grandpa, and Jed couldn't help laughing at Bill's wild antics. But Liza was caught up in thoughts of her own. She had

148

opened the package marked "Mary." Before her lay the deerskin doll.

"Ooh," squealed Liza. Gently she picked up the doll to get a better look at her. Brown beaded eyes met Liza's blue ones.

The others heard Liza squeal and came over to her.

"Oh, she does have real hair!" said Liza touching each long black braid. "And look at those little beaded moccasins!"

"Blue Feather," whispered Grandpa.

"What did you say, Grandpa?" asked Liza.

"Blue Feather, I just remembered," said

Grandpa. "That's the name Aunt Mary gave the doll. There used to be a blue feather in her hair."

Liza picked up the wrappings she had taken from around the doll. She looked through them quickly.

"Here it is! Here it is!" she said, holding up a small blue feather. Liza stuck the feather in the doll's hair.

"There you are, Blue Feather," said Liza happily. She hugged the doll softly.

"Hey, Jed," said Bill, "what's wrong with you?"

Then everybody noticed that Jed was still holding the other package.

"I-I thought maybe Grandpa would want to open this one," said Jed. "It's the one his father was meant to have."

Grandpa quickly went over to Jed. He put an arm around Jed's shoulder and said,

"What! Take away the fun I'm having watching you! Nonsense, boy. Open that package."

In an instant Jed had the paper off and was holding a large leather shield.

"Gee," he said, then whistled. "Look at that, would you?"

"Yes, sir," said Grandpa. "That's a real battle picture."

"I'd sure like to have that!" said Bill. "I'll trade with you."

"Oh, no you won't," said Jed. "You have what you said you wanted. Isn't that right, Grandpa?"

Grandpa didn't answer. Jed looked around for him. He was surprised to find Grandpa on his knees looking into the empty pillar.

"What's the matter, Grandpa?" he asked. "Did we miss something?"

"No, no," said Grandpa. "I just wanted to see how this thing was made. It's like a regular safe. Those things would have kept forever in this. And to think, nobody ever knew it was here!"

Suddenly Liza jumped up.

"Oh," she said, "I felt a raindrop. I can't let Blue Feather get wet."

Liza ran to the house. The others quickly followed her as the raindrops peppered the ground all around.

"That was a real surprise shower," said Grandpa.

"You know," said Jed, "it was raining the night you told us the two stories."

"And it was because of the rain that we were inside the day we found the first clue," said Liza.

"Now we're inside again because it's raining," said Bill. He looked up at the old picture.

"Say, Grandpa," he said, "are you sure there's not more to that story?"

"No, it's a finished story now," said Grandpa. "You children have written the last chapter. I'm mighty proud of you."

"But, Grandpa," said Liza, "you will still tell us the story, won't you?"

"Huh!" said Gran. "You would think

your Grandpa was the only person around here with a story to tell."

The children turned to Gran in surprise.

"Gran," said Jed, "do you have a story?"

Gran's eyes twinkled. She said, "I just might. But it will have to wait. You know what your Grandpa's grandmother said. Work must come before play. And, it's time to fix lunch."

"Aw, Gran!" said the children.

Grandpa chuckled loudly. The children looked at him and began to laugh, too. And they all followed Gran to the kitchen to help fix lunch.

M2

1/B3